H.G. Wells
THE WAR OF THE WORLDS

essay by
Joshua Miller

The War of the Worlds
Originally published as Classics Illustrated no. 124

Adaptation by Henry Miller
Art by Lou Cameron
Cover by Clem Robins

For Classics Illustrated Study Guides
computer recoloring by VanHook Studios
editor: Madeleine Robins
assistant editor: Valerie D'Orazio
design: Joseph Caponsacco

Classics Illustrated: War of the Worlds © Twin Circle Publishing Co., a division of Frawley Enterprises; licensed to First Classics, Inc. All new material and compilation © 1997 by Acclaim Books, Inc.

Dale-Chall R.L.:7.65

ISBN 1-57840-188-7

Classics Illustrated® is a registered trademark of the Frawley Corporation.

Acclaim Books, New York, NY
Printed in the United States

THE WAR OF THE WORLDS

By H. G. WELLS

*T*OWARD THE END OF THE NINETEENTH CENTURY, SEVERAL NEWSPAPERS IN ENGLAND CARRIED A SMALL ACCOUNT OF THE DISCOVERY OF A MASS OF FLAMING GAS, CHIEFLY HYDROGEN, ORIGINATING ON THE PLANET MARS AND MOVING WITH ENORMOUS SPEED TOWARD THE EARTH.

THE NEWS ITEM, HOWEVER, WAS SO INSIGNIFICANT, THAT I, AS WELL AS THE REST OF THE WORLD, IGNORED WHAT PROVED TO BE ONE OF THE GRAVEST DANGERS THAT EVER THREATENED THE HUMAN RACE.

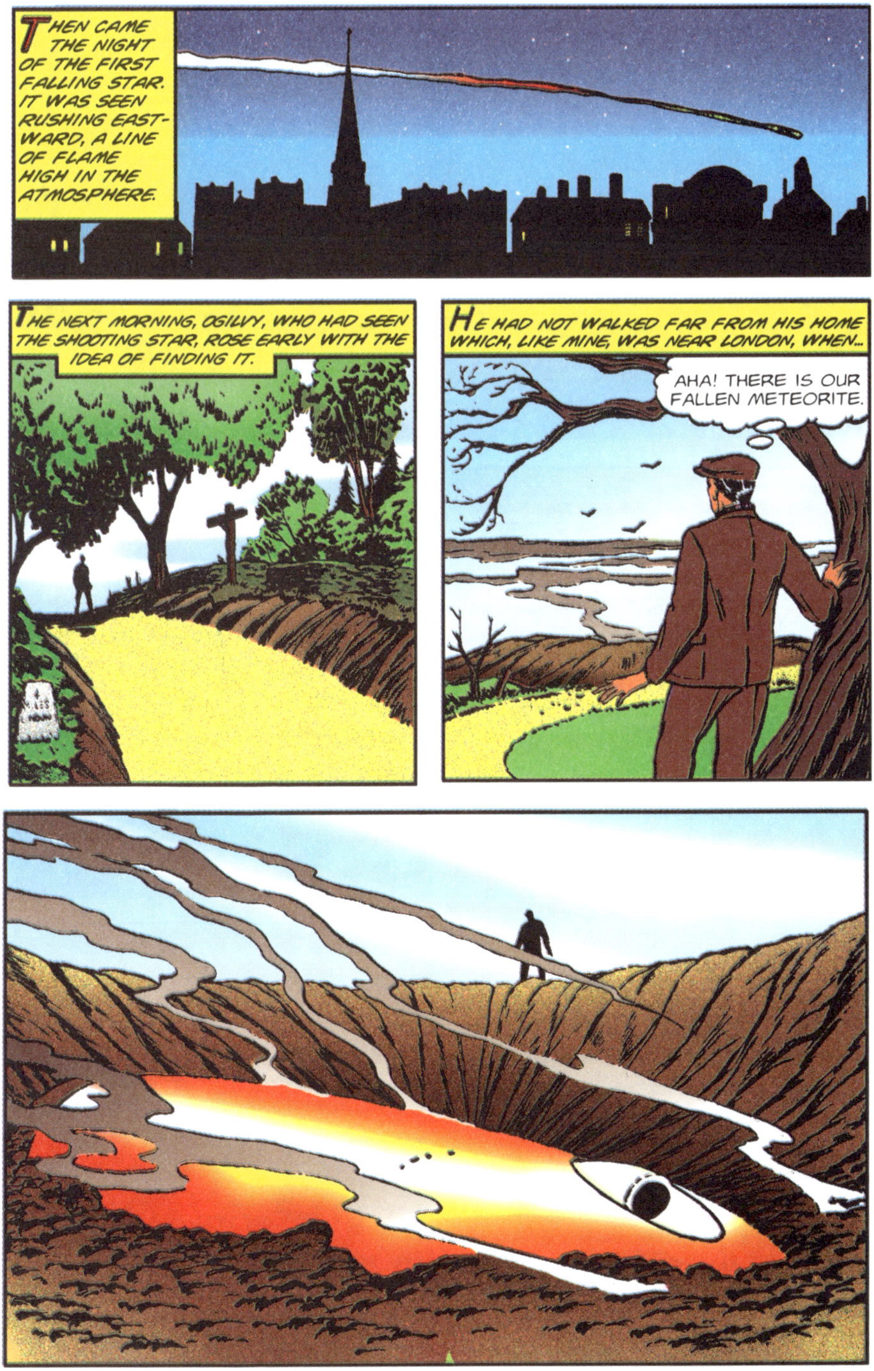

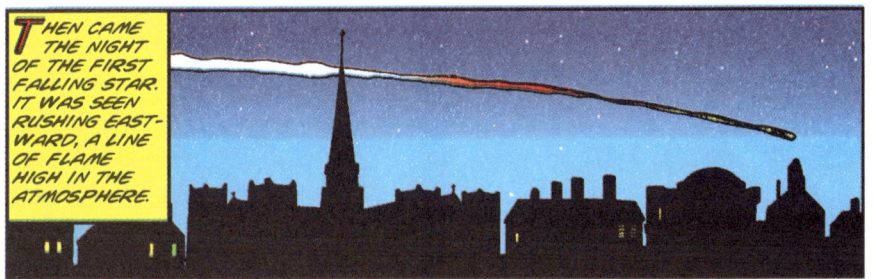

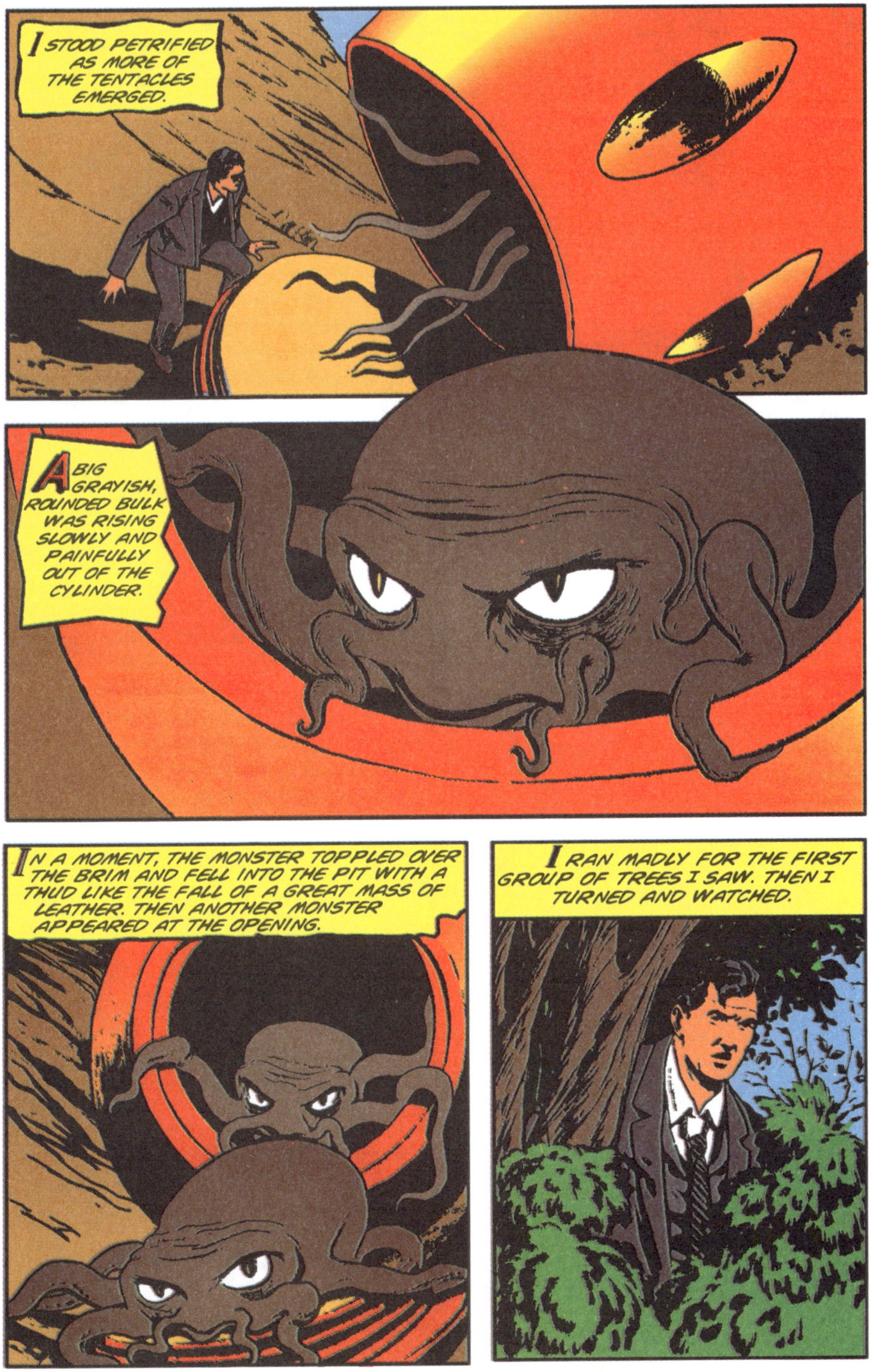

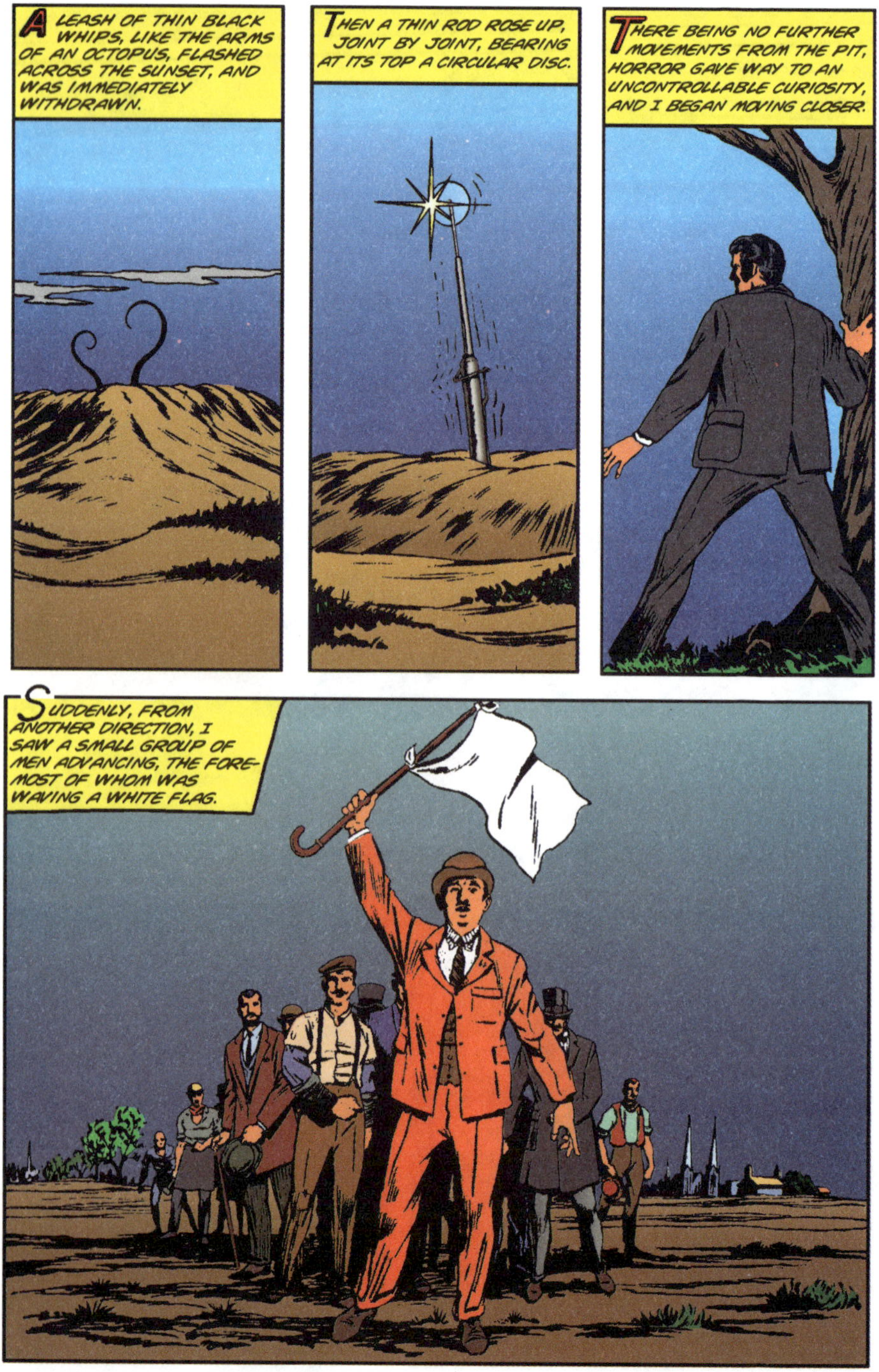

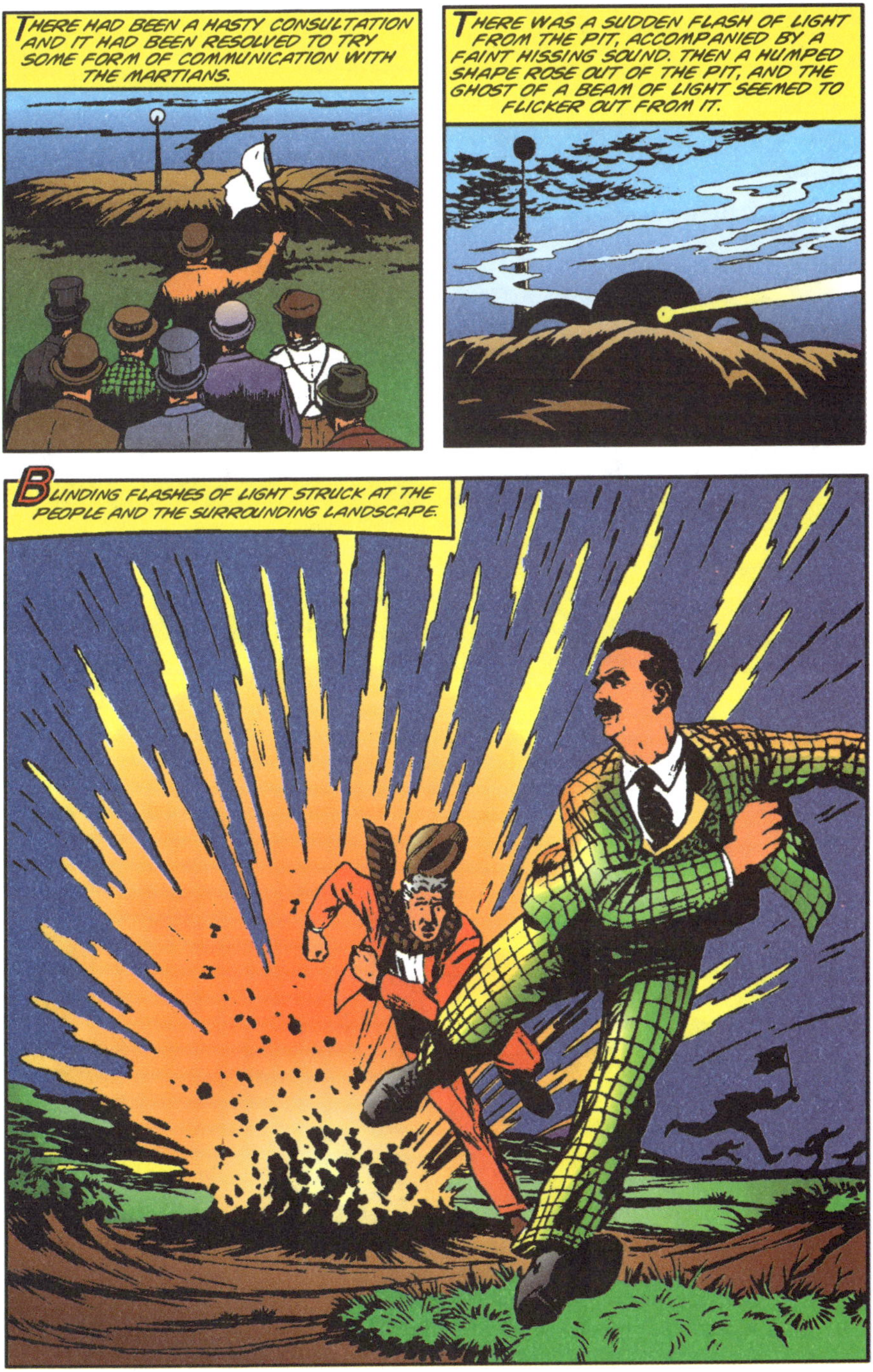

THEY HAVE DONE A FOOLISH THING. THEY ARE DANGEROUS, BECAUSE, NO DOUBT, THEY ARE MAD WITH TERROR. A SHELL FIRED INTO THE PIT, IF WORST COMES TO WORST, WILL KILL THEM ALL.

BUT, GROWING CONFIDENT WITH WINE AND GOOD FOOD, I OVERLOOKED ONE THING.

THE MARTIANS POSSESSED SUCH MECHANICAL INTELLIGENCE THAT THEY WERE ABLE TO OVERCOME THE PROBLEM OF GRAVITY. BACK AT THE SAND PIT, THEY WORKED ON THE MACHINES THEY WERE MAKING READY.

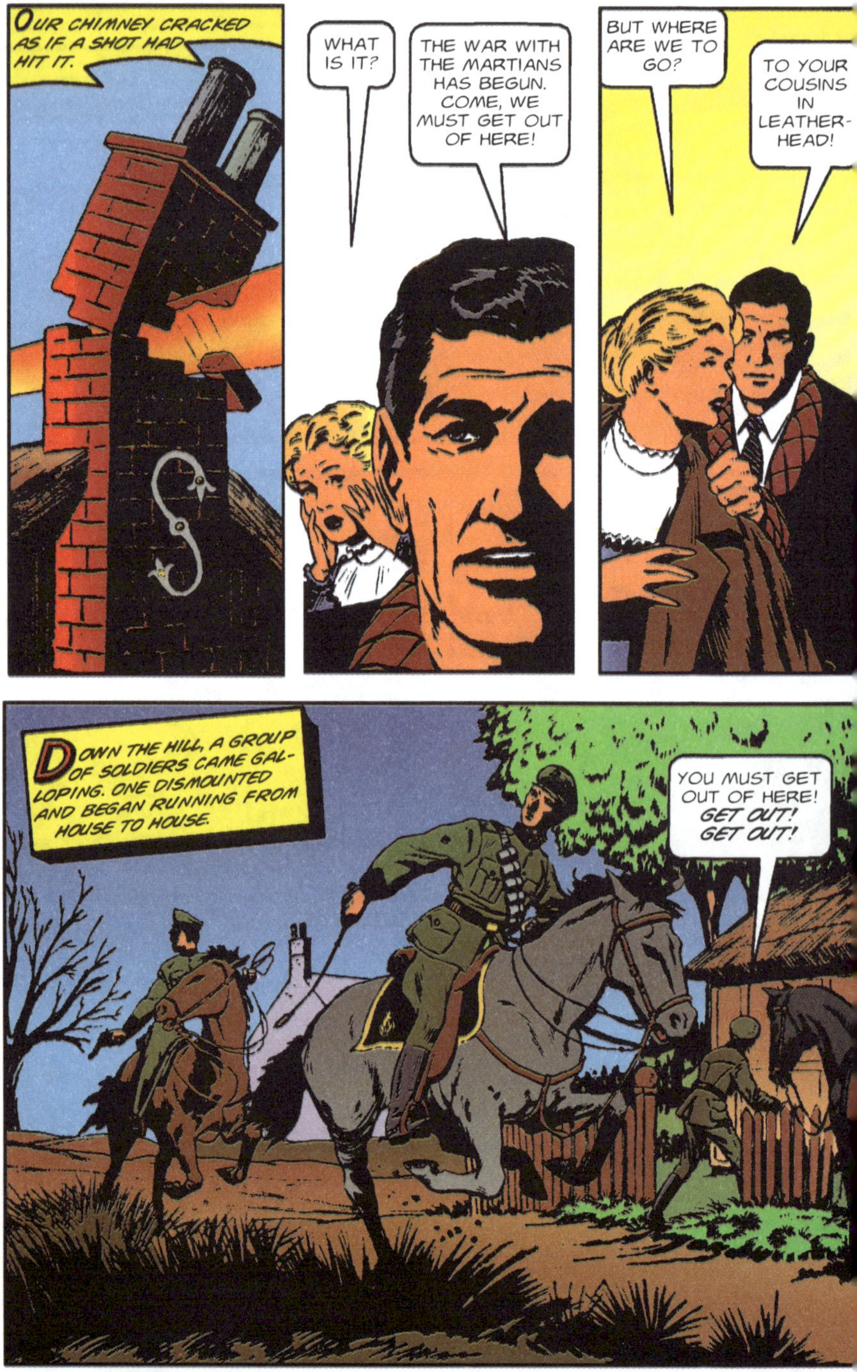

The monster joined its companion half a mile away. They both stooped over something in the field, which I suspected was the third cylinder I had just seen fall.

I managed to elude the monsters, and arrived exhausted at my home.

I ate some food and changed my clothes. Then I went to my study and stared out of the window.

"I LAY STILL, SCARED OUT OF MY WITS. MOST OF THE COMPANY HAD BEEN WIPED OUT AROUND ME."

I LAY THERE FOR A LONG TIME. HOW I MANAGED TO EVADE THE MARTIANS, I DON'T KNOW. I DON'T EVEN REMEMBER HOW I GOT HERE.

WE LOOKED OUT OF THE STUDY WINDOW. THREE OF THE METALLIC GIANTS STOOD ABOUT THE PIT, SURVEYING THE DESOLATION THEY HAD MADE. THEN THEY TURNED AND MARCHED OFF IN THE DIRECTION OF LONDON.

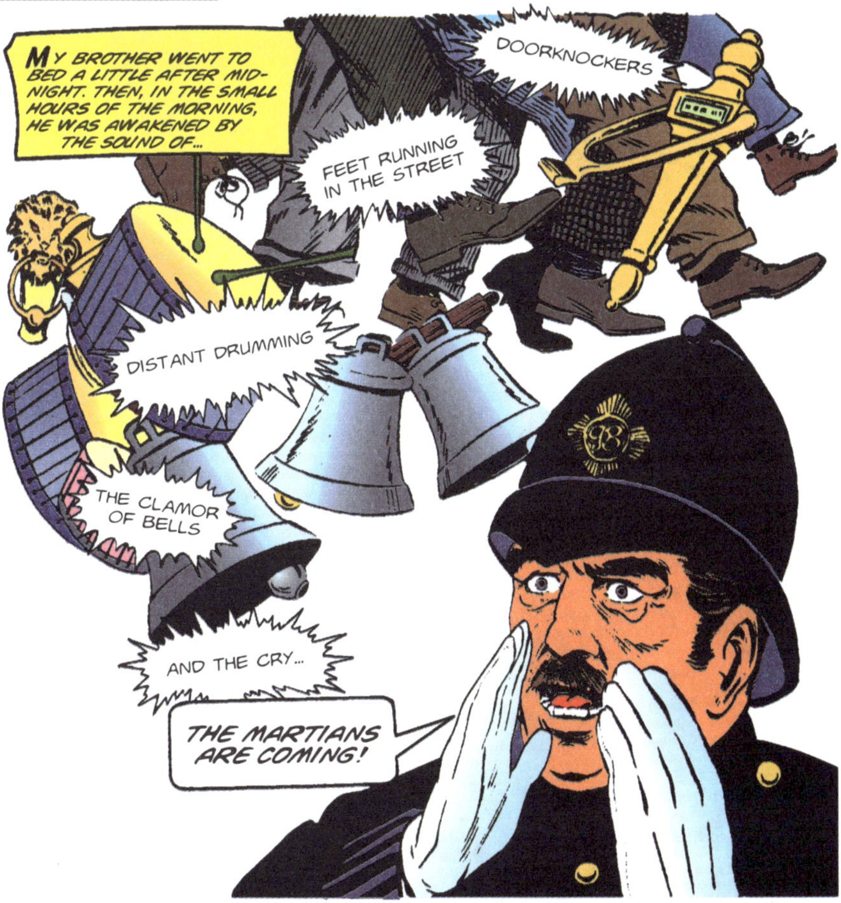

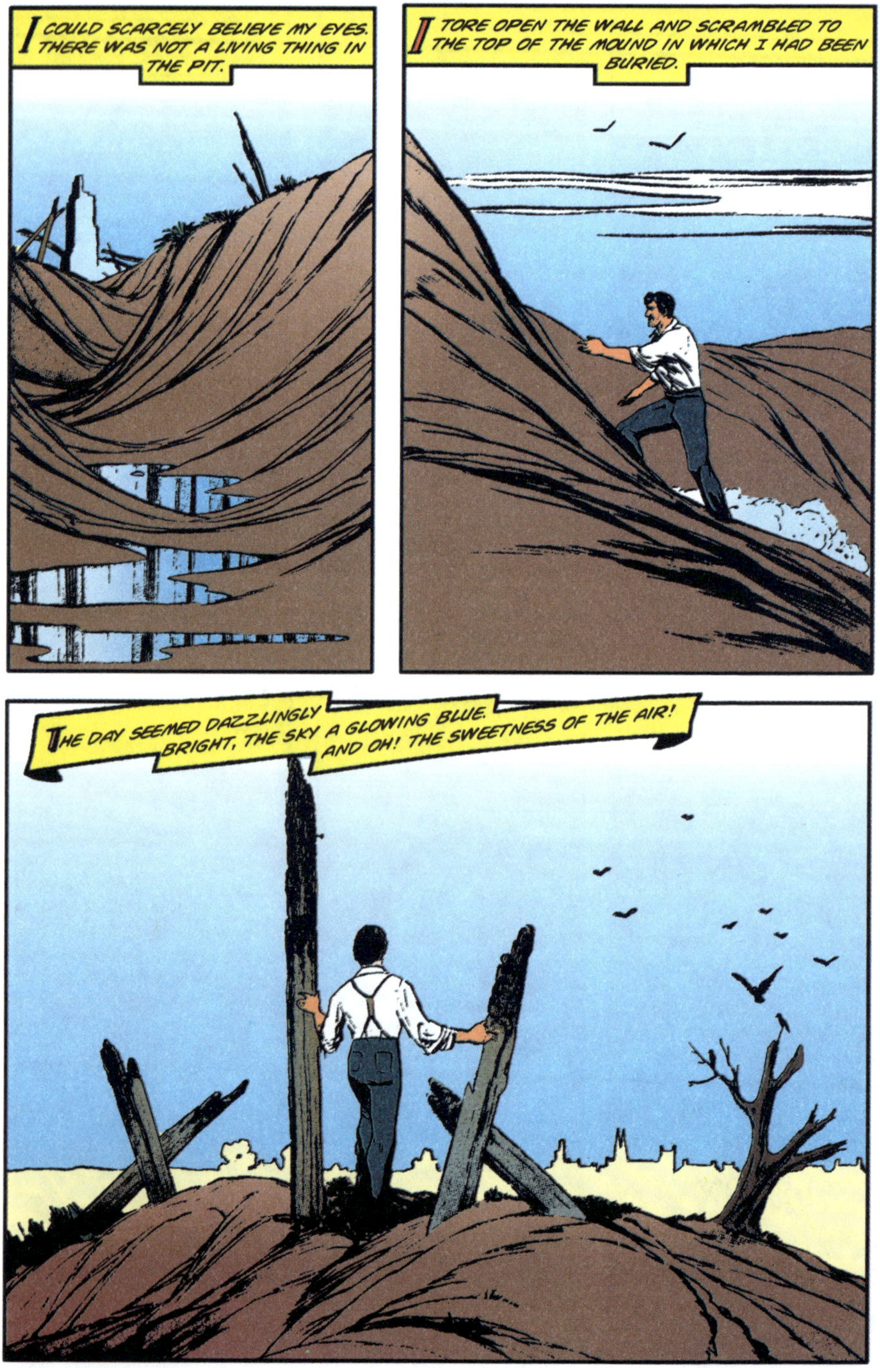

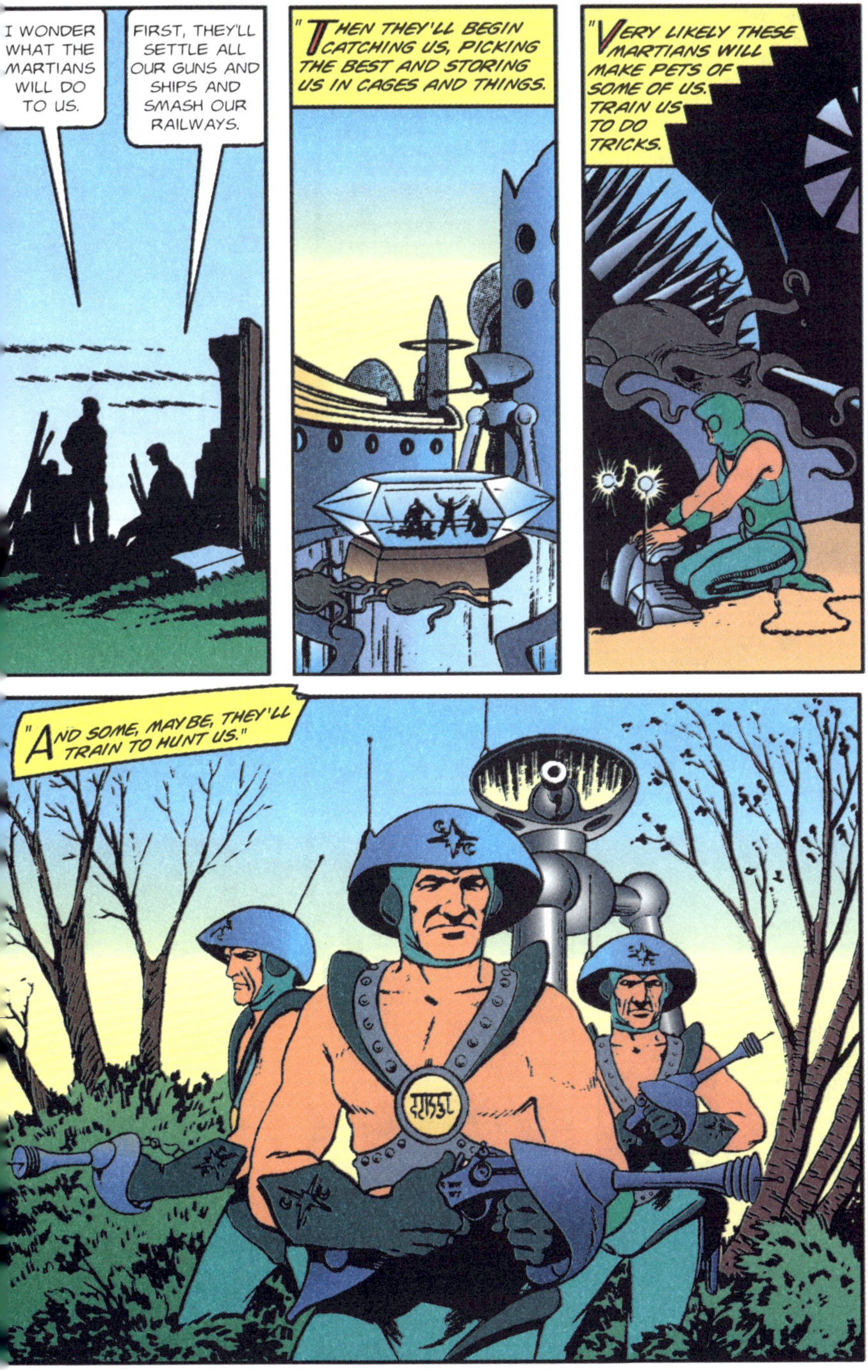

I RAN RECKLESSLY TOWARD THE MONSTER. THEN I CAME UPON A SCENE I WILL NEVER FORGET.

THE MARTIANS WERE DEAD EVENTUALLY, I REALIZED THEY HAD BEEN SLAIN BY THE HUMBLEST THINGS THAT GOD, IN HIS WISDOM, HAD PUT UPON THIS EARTH.

THE MARTIANS HAD BEEN SLA(IN) BY DISEASE BACTERIA AGAINST WHICH THEIR SYSTEMS WERE TOTALLY UNPREPARED. THERE ARE NO BACTERIA ON MARS, AND AS SOON AS THE INVADERS ARRIVED ON EARTH, OUR MICRO SCOPIC ALLIES BEGAN TO WOR(K) THEIR OVERTHROW. MAN HAS DEVELOPED AN IMMUNITY TO THESE GERMS. BY THE TOLL OF BILLION DEATHS, HE HAS BOUGH(T) HIS BIRTHRIGHT TO THE EARTH FOR MEN NEITHER LIVE NOR DI(E) IN VAIN.

THE WAR OF THE WORLDS

H.G. Wells

As the nineteenth century faded into the twentieth, many people feared that catastrophe was imminent. In 1898, H.G. Wells drew on this widespread fear in his gripping novel, *The War of the Worlds*. Pitting human science against hyper-intelligent invaders from Mars, Wells dramatized an event that has fascinated Earthlings for centuries. Who among us hasn't wondered whether living creatures exist somewhere in the cosmos, and whether they would see humans as friends or enemies?

This may be an especially good time to read (or re-read) Wells' book and to understand the anxieties of his first readers. One hundred years after the first publication of *The War of the Worlds*, we face similar fears as the twentieth century *and* the second millennium draw to a close. Now, as in Wells' time, concern about the future turns our eyes upward, to the endless universe. Astronomers continue to probe the sky for signs of living beings in our solar system and beyond. Meanwhile, reports of alien landings on Earth continue to emerge from all corners of the globe. The most dramatic recent event connected to beings from the outer reaches of space was the mass suicide among members of a cult called Heaven's Gate, who expected to join an interstellar "mother ship" after death. But the Heaven's Gate cultists aren't alone; others still await alien landings. And who can say for sure that Earthlings are the only sentient life forms in existence?

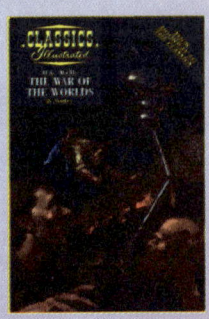

THE AUTHOR

H.G. Wells is known today as the author of some of the earliest, and most exciting, science fiction. But Wells was also the author of philosophical, historical, educational, and scientific works; in all, he wrote over a hundred books. In his lifetime, Wells was thought of as one of the most outspoken writers on the political and moral issues of his time. Today, though, we read him primarily as the author of some of the most startling novels about the future ever written.

Herbert George Wells was born in a suburb of London on September 21, 1866. His father maintained a small sports-equipment or hardware store, and was also a professional cricket player. His mother was a devoutly religious woman who had worked as a domestic servant before marrying. Wells' mother tried to convince the young H.G. (called "Bertie" as a child) of her religious convictions, but he remained steadfastly skeptical throughout his life. Physically and philosophically, he was more like his thoughtful, industrious, active father.

When he was seven years old, Wells

broke his leg in a fall. He was bed ridden for weeks, and his father brought him biology and astronomy textbooks to read. Later in life, Wells thought of those days spent reading in bed as a child as the beginning of his scientific fascination with the workings of the human body and of the universe. Since his father's professions were not profitable enough to support the family's three sons (H.G. was the youngest), in 1880 his mother went back to work as a live-in housekeeper. H.G. worked briefly as a draper's assistant, then as a tutor, and finally as a teacher at a grammar school.

After teaching for a year (1883-4), Wells received a scholarship to study physics, biology, and other sciences in London. He remained there for three years, deepening his understanding of anatomy and astronomy. By the time he had completed his studies, Wells was convinced of the importance of science in understanding the modern world. At the same time, he read widely in literature and gave his cynical skepticism vent in humorous articles published in a student newspaper. When he left the university, he returned to teaching.

A second major injury changed his life when a severe kick—while playing soccer—crushed one of his kidneys. For four months, Wells was confined to his bed and he spent much of the time writing. He returned to London in 1888, poor, but determined to live as a writer and a thinker. While teaching, he wrote scientific articles and textbooks on biology and physiography. When he turned his pen to satirical essays, Wells found that he could earn more money as a full-time writer than as a teacher.

Throughout the 1890s Wells wrote a series of articles that brought him a comfortable income, as well as a certain measure of fame. In 1895, he published his first novel, *The Time Machine*, which began his long career as a writer of fantasy and speculation. Novel followed novel and he rapidly published *The Island of Dr. Moreau* (1896), *The Invisible Man* (1897), and *The War of the Worlds* (1898). By the time *The War of the Worlds* appeared, Wells' name was a familiar one in British literary and philosophical circles.

Wells began writing *The War of the Worlds* in the summer of 1895 and completed it toward the end of 1897. The ideas that underlie the novel, however, were with Wells long before that. As a student of the sciences and an avid reader of philosophy, ten years earlier he had imagined a future in which humans' knowledge would be so great that they evolved into enormous brains with hands. But Wells credited his brother Frank with the suggestion to dramatize an invasion of Earth by beings from another planet.

The War of the Worlds appeared first as a serial in Pearson's Magazine (in 1897), and later as a book in England and the United States (1898). Wells published continuously into the twentieth century on subjects as diverse as history, biography, autobiography, utopianism, and biological evolution. He also wrote for film and radio productions.

From 1944 on, Wells' health declined significantly and quickly. In his last years, he lived largely as an invalid. H.G. Wells died on August 13, 1946.

CHARACTERS

Among its other oddities, *The War of the Worlds* is a highly unusual work in that there is almost no plot to speak of and it has few characters of substance. The setting (1890s England) and the narrator's long descriptions largely tell the story themselves. Nevertheless, readers must pay attention to the cast of characters in *The War* in order to catch Wells' broader aims for the novel.

The Martians are clearly the stars of this story. Unnamed and barely described, the super intelligent beings have left their home on Mars, forced to abandon it as the planet dries out and becomes uninhabitable. They have chosen Earth as their new home and they invade in order to capture the surface of the planet as a new home and the humans as a source of food.

According to the narrator's description, the Martians appear physically like octopuses with a huge head and sixteen tentacles around a small, fleshy mouth. They have large, dark eyes, but no nose. These almost bodiless creatures don't exactly eat; they feed themselves by injecting blood from other organisms.

The Martians arrive on Earth in cylinders that the humans mistake, at first, fo meteors. Even though the Earth's denser atmosphere should make movement mor difficult, the Martians are well-equipped Hiding in the cylinders, they build enormous machines in which they can destro whole cities. Their Fighting Machines a at least one hundred feet high with three legs that can maneuver over hills and through deep waterways.

The Martians have two weapons. The first is a Heat Ray that can sizzle anything i its path. With this explosive and absolut ly precise weapon, the Martians ca destroy peo ple, buildings, even whole cities if they choose to. Their sec ond weapon is the ominous Black Smoke which kills every human that it reaches. The Martians use the smoke rather than the Heat R in London, presumably in order t kill the inhabitants without havin to destroy the city's buildings and other large structures.

But even the strongest invader may overlook some crucial fact and the Martians neglect to protect themselves from Earth's bacteria. Where humanity can't turn back t Martian onslaught, the "di ease bacteria against which

Do the Martians Really Look Like Octopi?

The Classics Illustrated edition emphasizes the octopus like appearance of the Martians. But, if anything, the Martians as H.G. Wells describes them are even more terrifying than the pictures can show. As the Narrator says, "those who have never seen a living Martian can scarcely imagine the strange horror of its appearance." This idea of "strange horror" in the Martian's appearance is very important to Wells.

When the Narrator first spies the Martians struggling to climb out of the a cylinder, he does not even know that there are living creatures within. The first thing that he sees in the darkness is a pair of "luminous discs—like eyes." Then he thinks that he sees a snake-like object, but that turns out to be only one small arm of a being "the size, perhaps, of a bear." Once he sees the entire Martian, the Narrator is struck dumb:

> Two large dark-coloured eyes were regarding me steadfastly. The mass that framed them, the head of the thing, was rounded, and had, one might say, a face. There was a mouth under the eyes, the lipless brim of which quivered and panted, and dropped saliva. The whole creature heaved and pulsated convulsively.

In Wells' description, the "greyish" Martians are similar in appearance to octopi, with sixteen (instead of eight) tentacles around a large head. The Narrator seems most fascinated by "the extraordinary intensity of the immense eyes" that watch him.

Much later, when the Narrator is watching the Martians from his hiding spot (with the Curate) in an abandoned house, he notes "their huge round bodies—or, rather, heads—about four feet in diameter." On their faces, they have "no nostrils" but just the huge eyes and a "fleshy beak" of a mouth.

Both times that the Narrator sees the Martians, he stresses the elements of their physical appearance that he finds "unspeakably nasty." He wants to suggest that no words can describe the "ungovernable terror" that the Martians inspire in him. The "oily brown skin" that "glistened like wet leather" paralyzes the Narrator in "disgust and dread."

It's worth remembering when reading *The War of the Worlds* that the concept of the physically repulsive space alien isn't one that has existed forever. Twentieth-century novels, television, and film have used similar stereotypes of nasty and destructive interplanetary aliens, but Wells was one of the first to use this type of character. Only in more recent times have beings from other planets been portrayed as both cute and harmless (or even beneficial).

their systems were unprepared" delivers the fatal blow.

The most lasting significance of Wells' portrayal of invaders from Mars may be the fact that they are both physically grotesque and threatening to humanity. Science-fiction novels as well as horror films up to the present day draw on Wells' story when they depict absolute struggles between the human and the non human.

The Narrator of *The War of the Worlds* is the guiding figure of the work. It's through this unnamed speaker that we learn the story of the Martian invasion. We depend entirely on his observations and his assessments of the various events. What makes this fact a bit more complicated is that, as Wells hints at times, the Narrator isn't always correct in his judgments.

The Narrator is a writer and a philosopher who lives in the district of Surrey, where the first cylinder from Mars crashes to Earth. He sees this object plummeting to the ground and (like all others) assumes that it's a meteorite. Once he sees the cylinder itself, however, the Narrator is quick to realize the danger that the Martians present. Unlike the people around him, he does not ignore the power of the aliens' weapons.

But even he underestimates the Martians' intentions. By moving his wife to a nearby town, the Narrator thinks that she will be safe. Once the Martians begin using their Heat Ray, he realizes that no one will be safe from their march toward London.

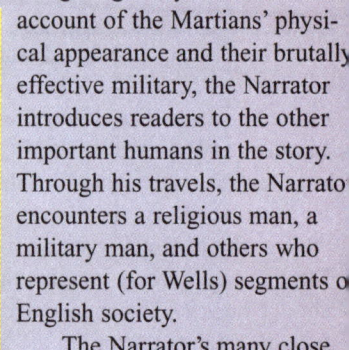

HAVEN'T YOU HEARD OF THE MEN FROM MARS? THE CREATURES FROM MARS?

In addition to recording the invasion of Earth and giving an eyewitness account of the Martians' physical appearance and their brutally effective military, the Narrator introduces readers to the other important humans in the story. Through his travels, the Narrator encounters a religious man, a military man, and others who represent (for Wells) segments of English society.

The Narrator's many close scrapes with the terrifying Martians suggest that he's nimble as well as lucky. He manages to view them from a nearby hiding spot and his observations are the only full account we have of their physical appearance.

At the same time, the Narrator is, at best, an accidental hero. He takes part in no battles, saves no lives, and even kills the cowardly Curate (an event that the CI edition omits). His most positive act is to take his wife to her cousins in Leatherhead, but that proves to be useless since the Martians later destroy the town. Remarkably, the final reunion between wife and husband, which ends the novel, occurs not because of the Narrator's actions but in spite of them!

When he finally reaches London, the Narrator finds that the Martians' Black Smoke has killed all of the humans who did not flee. Wandering through the deserted city, he realizes he doesn't see any Martians, either. Only then does he come upon the seventh (and final) cylinder, whose occupants are either already dead or near death as a result of terrestrial bacteria. He realizes that the Martians, though militarily superior, have lost their war for the Earth. He also concludes that his wife, whom he brought to "safety" in Leatherhead has likely died there. Stunned, he wanders unconsciously for three days, back toward his home in Surrey. There he finds his wife, safe and sound.

In an important epilogue, the Narrator sums up scientific advances that came from the Martian invasion and the mysteries that remain (such as the exact chemical composition of the Black Smoke and the Heat-Ray). But he also raises a more important question for those dwelling on Earth with the new knowledge that there are other living beings on other planets. A "question of graver and universal interest" is whether there will be "another attack from the Martians."

Even though he predicts that there won't be another attack, since the Martians have lost "a vast advantage in the failure of their first surprise," the Narrator notes that those on Earth can't afford to think only of their own planet from this moment onward. Humans will have to attempt space travel too and search for habitable environments on other planets in case of catastrophes on Earth. It's hard to discount the narrator's conclusions, in view of the twentieth century's preoccupation with flight!

Ogilvy is a well-known British astronomer who is the first to realize that the fallen "meteorite" is actually a Martian "cylinder." Ogilvy plays an important role in the story, even though he's around for only the beginning. As an astronomer, Ogilvy makes scientific judgments based on currently available knowledge. He is one of the first to recognize the possible importance of the meteorite, but he also assumes that he will be able to reason

with the aliens, raising a white flag and marching up to the cylinder. When the aliens kill Ogilvy (in a group of would-be peacemakers), they demonstrate for the first time one weapon in their arsenal: the "Heat Ray." From this point on, the scientists give way to the military. The humans give up any pretense of friendly communication and settle on fighting back. Neither tactic proves to be particularly successful.

It may be worth considering that, although the narrator himself is a scientist, almost every scientific prediction in this book is wrong. Ogilvy is a prominent astronomer, yet his presumptions about the Martians are clearly incorrect and he's among the first that they kill.

Henderson is a journalist from London whom Ogilvy finds after discovering the aliens' cylinder. Like Ogilvy, Henderson knows that his profession can play an important role in this event. As a journalist, Henderson is one of the few people in late nineteenth century England who can send information around the country (and the world) rapidly. Without computers, television, or even radio we have, the residents of Wells' time depend on newspapers to find out about important events. Newspapers play a major role in this story by transmitting information about the aliens. As is the case today, some of the stories in the newspapers are misleading, but they *do* warn Londoners of the approaching danger as Martians march toward the city.

However useful, in this story journalism (like science), isn't a purely beneficial element of society. Newspapers downplay the threat that the aliens pose at first; later, they inspire panicked riots in London with screaming headlines such as "Dreadful Catastrophe!" and "London in Danger!"

The Curate is an assistant clergyman of sorts. This particular man is weak, unintelligent, imprudent figure. The Curate represents one possible response to the Martians' invasion: surrender. To the scientific and secular narrator (and to Wells himself), the Curate's response to the Martian onslaught is dangerous, hypocritical, and possibly immoral.

Wells' opinion of organized religion can be deduced from his portrait of the Curate. From almost the first moment that the Narrator meets the Curate, difficulties arise. The religious man assumes that the Martian invasion is divine punishment for the evils of humanity. Since the punishment is final, the Curate does not struggle against invasion by "God's ministers," but quotes (apparently randomly) Biblical passages on death and destruction. "This must be the beginning of the end," he predicts, "The end! The great and terrible day of the Lord!"

While the two men rest in an abandoned house, another Martian cylinder lands right next to the house. This allows the Narrator a chance to spy on the Martians. But the panicked, half-starved, impatient Curate begins to attract the Martians' attention with his loud voice and inability to eat according to the rations of food left in the house.

When the incoherent Curate decides to cut his own terror short, walk out to the Martians, and allow them to kill him, the Narrator is forced to kill the Curate himself (or risk being caught by the Martians as well). He strikes the Curate, but the sounds attract the attention of the nearby Martians. One of their Handling Machines creeps inside and pulls the

Curate's body out of the house. The Narrator remains inside until the Martians have left.

Ultimately, the Narrator is disgusted with the Curate, who can't control his own appetites, and is so eager to surrender to the Martians. Sensing the Curate's timidity, the Narrator strengthens his resolve not to submit to the invaders.

The Soldier (or The Artilleryman, as he's called in the novel) offers the Narrator a better way to deal with the conquering Martians than the Curate's quivering surrender. But after a brief temptation, the Narrator decides that the Soldier's plan is ultimately no better than the clergyman's.

The Narrator meets the Soldier when he returns to his house after taking his wife to her cousins in Leatherhead. The Soldier is the sole survivor of an artillery troop which has been destroyed by the Martians' weapons. He brings the Narrator up to date on the most recent events in the war.

Much later, after the Martians have conquered the surrounding areas and London, the Narrator runs into the Soldier again. By this time, the Martians have easily destroyed everything in their path and their victory seems to be only a matter of time.

Unlike the Curate, who sees the Martian success as proof of human guilt and Divine punishment, the Soldier harbors dreams of an underground resistance after the Martians take control of Earth. The Soldier is a clever, imaginative visionary: rather than panicking at the idea of Martian rule on Earth, he's figured out a way of surviving under the new circumstances. The Narrator is immediately impressed by the Soldier's sense of self-preservation and intelligence.

The Soldier's plan is to create an underground resistance movement, literally below ground, in London's sewer system. In fact, he's digging a tunnel in the ground when the Narrator happens

upon him. The Soldier plans to recruit other humans in his brigade who will live underground until they can steal the Martians' Fighting Machines from them. Then the humans will turn the power of the Heat Ray back on to its inventors.

For a time, the Narrator finds the charismatic Soldier convincing. It does seem as if the Martians are winning the war. But he soon realizes that the Soldier's plan is a fantasy. Instead of digging the tunnel, the two men end up playing cards and eating the food that remains. The Narrator decides that the Soldier's plan is just another way of accepting defeat at the hands of the Martians. When the military man tells him that "it *is* up with humanity. . . . We're down; we're beat," the Narrator tells us that he himself "had not arrived at this fact." Instead, the Narrator "still held a vague hope" that the Martians could be beaten.

In the end, the Soldier—though resourceful and inventive—does not have the strength to follow his own plan. Like the man of science (Ogilvy) and the man of religion (the Curate), the man of war fails to come up with a realistic response to the Martians.

The Brother of the Narrator is a medical student in London. Since the Narrator spends most of the book outside of London, he uses his brother's observation to describe the Martian's march into London. The Medical Student's description of the mass panic and rioting in London when the news reaches there is one of the most memorable scenes in the story.

When the Martians reach London, they begin using the deadly Black Smoke instead of their destructive Heat Ray. "Setting about it as methodically as men might smoke out a wasps' nest," relates the

Narrator, "the Martians spread this strange stifling vapour over the Londonward country." And the strategy succeeds: Londoners pile into crammed railroad cars in hysterical attempts to leave the area. The Student steals a bicycle and rides out of the city center to the north. When one of the wheels breaks, he's forced to continue his journey by foot. He rescues two women from an angry mob that wants to steal their horse-drawn carriage and they return the favor by taking him away from the city.

The three reach a steamboat leaving England, but from the boat they observe a vicious battle between an armored gun ship and the huge Martian machines, which have walked right into the sea. Although the battleship manages to hit two of the giant machines, a blast of the Heat Ray destroys it entirely.

Just before his ship

loses sight of England, the Student is dumbfounded to see something flying upward in the sky. Knowing that the Martians know how to fly in the Earth's atmosphere is demoralizing to those (like the Narrator) who still think that humans can defeat the Martians. To make matters worse, the flying object seems to be dropping the deadly Black Smoke over London.

THEMES
What Kind of Story Is This?

The War of the Worlds is a difficult work to fit into the categories of traditional literature. Readers have referred to it in various ways, as fiction, science-fiction, fantasy, journalism, satire, philosophy, futurism, docudrama and even myth. Perhaps the most imaginative category created to describe much of H.G. Wells' work is the "scientific romance."

Whatever label one places on *The War of the Worlds*, one must take into account the ways in which Wells mixes fact with fiction throughout the novel. For example, many of the names that he uses are those of real people, alive and well-known when the book first appeared. Other names are invented, chosen simply because they sound common enough to slip by unnoticed. Another example is Wells' mention of flight. Although the novel predates the Wright Brothers' first successful flight in Kitty Hawk, North Carolina, by at least five years, Wells does predict that humans will learn to fly in the next century!

Science-fiction was a fairly new literature at the turn of the century, so Wells' readers were almost as confused by his novel in 1898 as we are today. One important influence on Wells and on scientific-fantasy literature in general was Jules Verne. Verne's best known works, *Around the World in 80 Days*, *A Voyage to the Center of the Earth* and *Twenty Thousand Leagues Under the Sea*, were published about thirty years before.

An American reviewer of *The War of the Worlds* hailed it in 1898 as part of "a new species of literary work." The reviewer called "the quasi-scientific novel" of Verne and Wells a mixture of "journalistic style" and scientific learning. The reviewer summed up the story as "an Associated Press dispatch, describing a universal nightmare." In a similar vein, another contemporary reviewer called the plot "on the whole... remarkably plausible... not as romance, but as realism."

WHILE THE BRIEF BATTLE LASTED, THE STEAMBOAT BEAT ITS WAY SEAWARD.

Why Do the Martians Attack Earth?

The other way of asking this question is, why don't the travelers from Mars accept the Earthlings' offers to communicate before setting off to kill them? To answer this, we have to decide why the Martians have come to Earth.

At the beginning of the novel, the

Narrator notes that (based on his most recent scientific research), Mars is older than the Earth and therefore, if life existed on Mars, it would have begun long before life appeared on this planet. Wells uses the common nineteenth century assumption (disproved in the twentieth) that Mars "has air and water and all that is necessary for the support of animated existence." Starting from this assumption, it follows that if life has existed on Mars longer than it has on Earth, then Martian life forms could be more intelligent and more "advanced" in science and technology than Earth's.

But Mars has cooled (the Narrator is quick to remind us that the Earth will someday too) and is rapidly becoming uninhabitable. The Narrator imagines the Martians "looking across space with instruments and intelligences such as we have scarcely dreamed of" to see a tempting, nearby planet "green with vegetation and grey with water." From Mars, the only option is to conquer Earth: "To carry warfare sunward is, indeed, their only escape from the destruction that generation after generation creeps upon them."

The key point, for the Narrator and for Wells, is that these hyper intelligent beings are likely to regard Earthlings with exactly the same contempt as humans have for ants or mosquitoes. The Narrator reminds his readers that humans aren't above the same behavior themselves, extinguishing entire groups of living beings. "Before we judge of them too harshly," he tells us, "we must remember what ruthless and utter destruction our own species has wrought, not only upon animals, such as the vanished bison and the dodo, but upon its own inferior races." Wells' use of the term "inferior races" contradicts his own point here, suggesting that he accepts the idea that some groups of people are more "advanced" than others. But his argument is that the British (his first audience, though we

The War of the Worlds, Take Two

If one ever needed convincing of the power and sheer drama of H.G. Wells' novel of a Martian invasion of Earth, an American actor and director with a strikingly similar name, immortalized it.

In July of 1938, Orson Welles, a relatively unknown actor, was hired by CBS Radio to host a program called *First Person Singular*. It was a show in which he would dramatize literary works for a weekly radio audience. From the beginning, Welles was fascinated by the possibilities of gripping the audience with apparently real, yet fantastic, stories. In the first episode, Welles produced the novel *Dracula*, playing the title role himself. The show was mildly successful and Welles (with a team of talented writers and an entire sound orchestra) produced weeks of shows based on works such as *Treasure Island*, *A Tale of Two Cities*, and *Sherlock Holmes*.

But on the night before Halloween, Welles and his writers decided to play a prank on the entire country. They adapted H.G. Wells' novel *The War of the Worlds* to the contemporary United States. Even as they kept the central idea of Wells' work and some of his language, they changed the names and rewrote the entire novel in the form of radio news bulletins. In October, 1938, Americans were already thinking about the possibility of all-out war in Europe, and radio was the only way to receive up-to-date information on the situation. Rewriting until almost the last minute, Welles wanted the performance to sound as immediate as possible.

The show ran for an hour, from 8 pm, at the same time as the enormously popular Charlie McCarthy program was running on another station. Not long after 8, a somewhat uninteresting singer was on the McCarthy show, and thousands of listeners changed the channel to an interrupted program and the news that Martians were on a destructive march in New Jersey. Many people listening to Welles found his adaptation funny, others thought it silly, but a few listened and believed it. They became terrified and, instantly, a mass panic led people to flee their homes and drive to what they thought would be safety from the wreckage.

By the midway point in the show, the Martians were described as occupying New York City and spraying their lethal black smoke throughout Manhattan. Hundreds of frantic phone calls jammed police stations, newspapers, and radio stations. By the end of the hour-long show, the trickster returned to the air to reassure his believing audience:

> *"This is Orson Welles, ladies and gentlemen, out of character to assure you that* The War of the Worlds *has no further significance than as the holiday offering it was intended to be. . . . that was no Martian. . . it's Halloween."*

But the damage was done. The next day, newspaper headlines reported that the "Fake Radio 'War' Stirs Terror Through U.S." and *The New York Times* announced that Welles had "Radio Listeners in Panic, Taking War Drama As Fact."

Of the many remarkable aspects of this event, the fact that thousands of people were willing to believe the dramatic story of a Martian landing suggests that fears about the end of the world survive, have even grown, in the twentieth century.

can include other Europeans and Americans in this today) have taken the same attitude toward African and Asian peoples as the Martians do toward Earthlings.

The Narrator's rhetorical question is never fully answered in the novel: "Are we such apostles of mercy as to complain if the Martians warred in the same spirit" as we do? In Christian terms, let those who are without guilt cast the first stone.

Millennialism

What does the end of the century have to do with this story? Although the numbering of years is an arbitrary act, the final years of each century seem to attract more than their share of anxiety about the future. The final years of the century act as a transition from one time period to another, even if the periods are labels as meaningless as "nineteenth century" and "twentieth." Whether one refers to it by the catchy French term, *fin de siecle*, or the English, "turn of the century," few living in 1890s England could entirely escape the end-of-century nervousness.

"Millennialism" comes from the word "millennium," which is a period of a thousand years. Millennialism and "Millennial fears" refer to the widespread belief that the end of the world will occur at the end of a century or millennium, and that all of humanity has to prepare for it. It's primarily a religious concept (and specifically a Christian one), but by no means are millennial anxieties limited to religious people. Deeply secular and even irreligious persons have been known to take extra measures to ward off the effects of "the end of all things."

Those who believe that the world will go out with a bang, not a whimper, may believe that spectacular events will

Becoming Alien

The first thing aspiring writers hear is that they should "write what they know." Obviously, that rule gets stretched a lot, otherwise most speculative or fantastic literature would go right out the window. Most writers are able to put themselves in the heads of other humans—to understand basic human motivations and emotions. But what kinds of emotions or motivations do *aliens* have? How can a writer fathom what goes on in the mind of a non-human creature? Obviously, writers since Wells have tried: from *ET* to *Star Trek* to the hundreds of SF books on bookstore shelves, there's no shortage of alien lifeforms. What are some of the techniques for "building a better alien?"

•**Work from the Outside In**. Some writers start with the world their aliens live in. Create a high-gravity world and you (necessarily) create aliens who are physically built to deal with high gravity. Would they be immensely strong? Would they be telekinetic (to avoid having to move in high gravity)? How about their psychology? How would life in a high-gravity environment shape a culture?

•**Focus on One Quality**. Most of the aliens in the Star Trek universe are built this way: the warlike Klingons are obsessed with honor; Vulcans are all intellect, with emotion rigorously suppressed. Building an alien this way allows you to take a human quality—pride, intellect, greed, suspicion—and explore it, pushing it so far that it becomes, well, *alien*.

•**Make Them Loveably Curious.** Dozens of aliens, from ET to Mork, have worked their way into our hearts by trying to figure out what's going on in our heads. The great thing about using an alien who's new to our culture as a viewpoint character is that the alien himself can show us things we've forgotten to notice. Of course, it helps if the alien is cute or funny; an alien with an aggressive curiosity (the sort who beams you up to the Mother Ship and performs unspeakable experiments) is unlikely to win a reader's heart.

•**Make Them Forbiddingly Advanced**. Another way of steering clear of an alien's inner life is to make the creature too advanced for primitive lifeforms like ourselves to understand. A writer creating this kind of alien can essentially tell the reader, "I'd explain about their motivations, but you wouldn't understand." Even the peaceful aliens are a little unnerving, just as a very big, smart, stern adult must be to a small child.

•**Make Them Unlovably Scary**. The Alien as Attacker has been a staple of science fiction since *The War of the Worlds*. The reader may never understand the alien's reason for attacking Earth in *War*, or *Independence Day,* or *The Thing* or *Invasion of the Body Snatchers*. The reason the alien in the *Alien* films goes after people may be mother love—or may be plain bloody-mindedness. In the final analysis, it doesn't matter. Scary Aliens stand for The Other, the people or things that are not like us, that cannot be understood because they're just *different*.

occur just before the very end. A massive Martian invasion would certainly fall into that category. In *The War of the Worlds* (published in 1898), the Curate's steadfast belief (much to the Narrator's annoyance) that the Martians herald the end of the world is one example of millennial panic.

Millennialism does not appear only at the end of the centuries (or millennia). Great fears about "the end" arise during times of radical change or great uncertainty. Large wars especially stoke millennial fears. (For one of the most spectacular examples of millennialism occurring in the middle of a century, see **War of the Worlds: Take Two**)

So what is Wells suggesting about these worries about the end of the world? The novel provides at least three responses to the Martian attack: the Curate's, the Soldier's, and the Narrator's. Both the Curate and the Soldier hold viewpoints that amount—in H.G. Wells' view—to surrender. Both of them take for granted that the world as they know it is ending and a new one (Heaven or Hell for the Curate; Martian rule for the Soldier) is beginning.

But the Narrator's view may be the crucial one. At the beginning of the novel, he tells us he's a philosopher and a writer. But throughout the story he "tries on" the beliefs of others: while with the Curate, he tries to understand the clergyman's perspective (until he realizes that the demented man is endangering them both). While with the Soldier, the Narrator is initially enthusiastic about his plan for fighting the Martian warriors from underground. Only when this plan becomes entirely unrealistic does the Narrator abandon it.

In the end, the Narrator's central goal is simple survival. He is the anti-millennial character of the novel, arguing that the end of the world is still a long time off. He considers the possibility that the others may be right, then leaves their fears behind in his belief that the war will be won.

Does the Setting Matter?

It's easy to overlook the issue of the setting in *The War of the Worlds*, but setting is crucial to the book. Even though the novel claims to be about the war for the future of the World, the entire story takes place in southern England. This matters a great deal when readers try to understand Wells' aims for the novel.

THE MARTIANS WERE SETTING FIRE TO EVERYTHING WITHIN RANGE OF THEIR HEAT RAY.

In an 1896 letter to a friend, Wells mentions a story-in-progress in which " completely wreck and destroy Woking," the town in which he was then living. I the letter, he continues to detail his joy in sacking London and its outlying suburbs through fiction. His choice of scenery is in no way accidental, but the meaning of the English backdrop for this story has been hotly debated since the work was first published. (See previous page).

Because the author chooses to make southern England the scene for the entire Martian landing, all of the central characters are British and all of "Earth's" armies are actually England's. To begin with, Wells' choice of location for the war presumes that England (and not even all of England, but only Southern England) is the battleground on which Earth's civilization will be won or lost.

Some readers have felt that Wells' imagined invasion of England by "aliens" might be a commentary on England's colonization of parts of Africa, Asia, and the Middle East. In this context, the Curate's strangely guilty interpretation of the Martians as "God's ministers" arriving to hand out divine punishment becomes more understandable. Considering its extensive colonial holdings across the globe, England (in particular) would have reason to be concerned about what it would receive in any system of ultimate justice.

Another view some critics have raised is that Wells was tapping into 1890s English anxieties that their neighbors to the east (France and Germany) and to the west (particularly the U.S.) were gaining in strength at the precise moment when England was growing weak. The decline of English military and political domination was a source of great concern at this point among British politicians and writers. A number of novels toward the end of the nineteenth century depicted an England in danger of invasion, but none did so quite as vividly as *The War of the Worlds*, with its scenes of flattened towns and the ghostly capital:

> *The farther I penetrated into London, the profounder grew the stillness of suspense, of expectation. . . . It was a city condemned and derelict. . . . The windows in the white houses were like the eye sockets of skulls. About me my imagination found a thousand noiseless enemies moving.*

Finally, another way of looking at the novel is that Wells was simply using the massive war as a way to satirize British prejudices and stereotypes. From this perspective, both the Curate and the Soldier appear to be more silly than dangerous. Each of them represents a form of intolerance, religious on the one hand and nationalistic on the other. Even the Narrator might appear a bit ridiculous, racing around the country without doing anything other than observing the Martians from various locations. He may simply be a parody of the Intellectual who is prone to think rather than to act.

This reading of the story makes sense of the rather prim lady whom the Medical Student (the Narrator's brother) saves from an unruly crowd. As she and the Student prepare to sail away from England (since remaining, by this point, appears to ensure death), she tells him that "she had never been out of England before" and "she would rather die than trust herself friendless in a foreign country." The brother notes that for this "poor woman," apparently "the French and the

Martians might prove very similar." Just in case readers didn't pick up on it earlier, Wells clearly wants to make sure that the pun of "aliens" from outer space and "aliens" as non-citizen residents of a nation is clear!

STUDY QUESTIONS

•If you were reviewing *The War of the Worlds* today, what category would you put it in? Is it realism, romance, or satire? Can you come up with a term that would include a few of these terms (or other terms)?

•Why do the Martians attack the Earth without making an attempt at sending—or receiving—friendly communication? Is it simply because they can? Do you agree with Wells' analogy between Martians and Humans on the one hand and European-American colonization of this planet on the other?

•Do you see millennialism at work in today's world? Where? Are modern forms of millennialism similar to or different from those Wells describes in *War of the Worlds?*

•How would the story of *The War of the Worlds* change if the setting was different? Would he have to change the story if the alien invasion took place in the U.S.? In China? Australia? Africa? Why don't the Martian cylinders land all over the globe at once? If they want to conquer Earth, why would they land only in England?

•Why do you think that Wells presents Martians who destroy the Earth without a second's thought, rather than kinder beings? What is he trying to show through the Martians' rampage of destruction? What examples can you find of the reverse? Can you compare Wells' terrifying aliens with cuter or kinder ones?

"And some, maybe, they'll train to hunt us."

•Many other social groups aren't represented in this novel and it may be worth considering in what context they might appear. (No politicians, no aristocracy, no women to speak of, no workers...)

About the Essayist

Joshua Miller is an instructor in the Department of English and Comparative Literature at Columbia University. He holds an M.Phil degree from Columbia.